AF269587

# FAMILIES of Fame & Fortune

## THE
# SMITHS

by Kristin J. Russo

## The Smiths
Families of Fame and Fortune



Full Tilt Press
42964 Osgood Road
Fremont, CA 94539
readfulltilt.com

Full Tilt Press publications may be purchased for educational, business, or sales promotional use.

**Editorial Credits**
Design and layout by Sara Radka
Edited by Renae Gilles
Copyedited by Nikki Ramsay

**Image Credits**
Getty Images: Allsport/Ezra O. Shaw, 25 (bottom), Blue Jeans Go Green/Michael Buckner, 24, Bryan Bedder, 17 (bottom), Carlos Alvarez, 15, Environmental Media Association/Jerod Harris, 16, Environmental Media Association/Randy Shropshire, cover, Environmental Media Association/Rick Polk, 21, 28 (left), Fox Broadcasting Company/Bryan Bedder, 27 (top), Frazer Harrison, 13 (bottom left), 25 (top), Haute Living/Alexander Tamargo, 12 (bottom), Kevin Winter, 3 (top), 7, 12 (top), 13 (middle), Michael Ochs Archives, 11, 26 (top), MJ Kim, 9, MTV/Kevin Winter, 20, People.com/Mike Coppola, 17 (top), Rich Fury, 5, 13 (bottom right), Stephen Lovekin, 8, Stringer/Brenda Chase, 3 (bottom), 26 (bottom), Vince Bucci, 23; Newscom: IFTN/United Archives, 13 (top), 28 (right), ZUMA Press/NTB Scanpix/Serud, 3 (middle), 19; Pixabay: 27707, background, GDJ, 12 (background), kulala13, 27 (bottom)

ISBN: 978-1-62920-845-9 (library binding)
ISBN: 978-1-62920-857-2 (ePub)

# Contents

In May 2019, Will Smith's family gathered in Hollywood. It was for the **premiere** of Disney's *Aladdin*. The family celebrated Will's role in the blockbuster hit. He plays the genie.

Will's wife, Jada Pinkett-Smith, wore a genie outfit. It was in honor of the character Will played. Trey, Jaden, and Willow joined their parents on the red carpet. In fact, it was a purple carpet. The color change was a nod to the Arabian "magic carpet" featured in the film.

Cameras flashed, and the stars greeted fans. Will playfully teased Jaden for being late to the event. "Fifteen minutes!" Jaden shrugged with a smile.

For the Smith family, this purple carpet was the perfect spot to celebrate. They are committed to dreaming big. They work hard to make all their wishes come true.

**premiere:** the first time a movie or TV show is shown

*Aladdin* explores themes of confidence and self-worth. The Smith family models these values. "This is why I am an artist—to have a purpose to share messages that can help people," said Will.

# Chapter 1

# MEET THE SMITHS

Will Smith had his first lead role in a movie in 1993. He was already a famous TV star and musician. Since then, he has made more than 40 movies. His nickname is "Mr. July." This is because his action movies earn huge profits in the summer.

*Independence Day* came out in 1996. It earned more than $50 million during its first weekend. The next summer, *Men in Black* was released. The film earned just as much. Will is also known for quieter films. These movies are just as powerful. *The Pursuit of Happyness* and *Ali* earned him two Academy Award nominations.

Will says his parents taught him to work hard and always do his best. His parents taught Will and his siblings to keep trying even when they faced challenges. He and his wife, Jada, model this **work ethic** for their children.

**work ethic:** the idea that hard work is a good thing

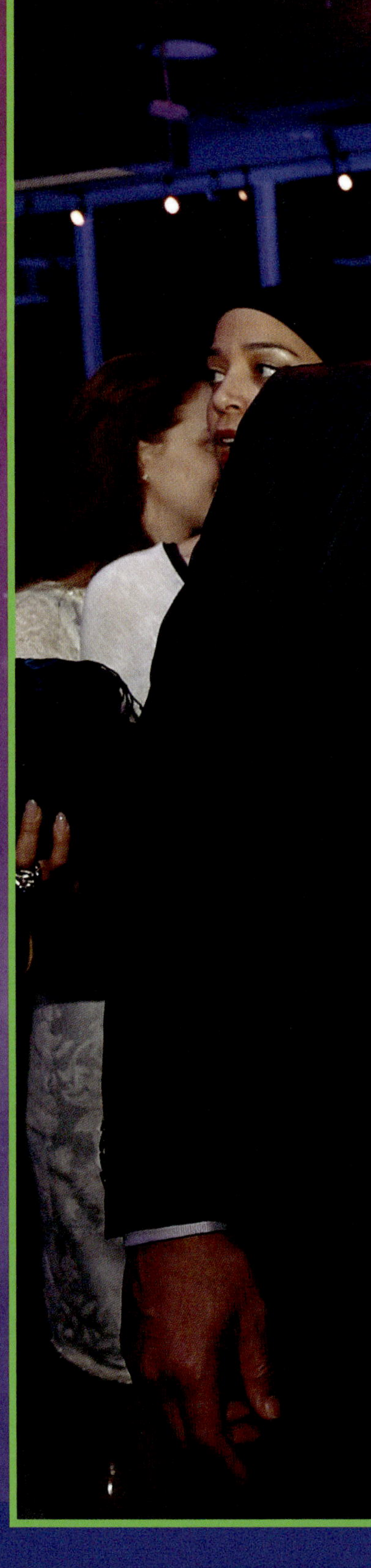

Will, Jaden, and Jada joined the cast and crew of Will's movie Focus for the premiere and after-party in 2015.

Famous Fact

Will Smith has won four Grammy Awards. He has been nominated for five Golden Globe Awards and earned two Academy Awards nominations.

Jada is a singer and writer. She is also a producer and actor. Jada has starred in several TV series. She has also been in more than 30 films. And that's not all. She hosts a Facebook Watch talk show too. It is called *Red Table Talk*. Jada and her mother, Adrienne Banfield-Jones, invite celebrity guests to their show. They tackle tough topics about life and work.

Willard Smith III is known as Trey. Will's first wife, Sheree Fletcher, is Trey's mother. They had Trey in 1992 and later divorced in 1995. Trey was a promising football player in college. Now he is an actor. He also performs as a **DJ** under the name AcE.

Jaden is Will and Jada's son. He is an actor, model, and **activist**. This means that Jaden gets involved with political issues. He takes action when he thinks events are unfair and rules should be changed.

Daughter Willow is an actor, singer, and model. The teen writes and produces much of her own music. She also works with her family on *Red Table Talk*.

**DJ:** someone who plays recorded music on a radio show or at a public gathering

**activist:** someone who works to support change in society

## WILL'S WORLD RECORD

On February 22, 2005, Will attended three red-carpet movie premieres in 24 hours. In Great Britain, he appeared at openings for his movie *Hitch* in Manchester, Birmingham, and London all on that day. No movie star had ever done that before. Will was entered into the Guinness Book of World Records for this feat.

# Chapter 2

# SMITH FAMILY HISTORY

Born in 1968, Will grew up in Pennsylvania. His parents named him Willard Carroll Smith Jr. They lived in a town called Wynnefield in West Philadelphia. Will was the second-oldest of four siblings. His sister, Pamela, is older. They have two younger twin siblings, Harry and Ellen. Will's father owned a refrigeration business. His mother was a school administrator.

### *Famous Fact*

Will's 1996 film *Independence Day* was about an alien invasion. It pulled in more than $817 million worldwide. This was Will's biggest box office hit until 2019, when *Aladdin* earned more than $1 billion.

Will's parents were tough but loving **taskmasters**. They wanted their four children to succeed. Once, Will's father tore down a brick wall. He wanted a new one in front of his refrigeration business. He told 12-year-old Will and his younger brother to rebuild it. It took the boys more than a year. But they finished. Later, Will said the experience taught him to believe that he can achieve his goals. It does not matter how challenging they are.

**taskmaster:** someone who assigns difficult work to other people

Jeff Townes and Will met in Philadelphia in the 1980s. They soon started making hip-hop music together as DJ Jazzy Jeff and the Fresh Prince.

Jada Koren Pinkett was born in 1971. She grew up in Baltimore, Maryland. Her mother was a nurse. Her father ran a construction company. They divorced when she was just a baby. Jada's grandmother helped to raise her and her brother, Caleeb.

Jada loved performing from a very early age. Her grandmother made sure she had dance and music lessons. Jada graduated from the Baltimore School for the Arts. Then she found success almost right away. She was cast in NBC's *A Different World*. It was a **sitcom** about college students. They went to a mostly African American university.

## Smith Family Tree

**Willard Carroll Smith Sr.**
*November 24, 1939–November 7, 2016*
refrigeration business owner

**Caroline Bright Smith**
school administrator

**Sheree (Zampino) Fletcher**
*November 16, 1967*
actress and producer

**Willard Carroll Smith Jr.**
*September 25, 1968*
musician and actor

**Willard Carroll "Trey" Smith III**
*November 11, 1992*
actor and DJ

**sitcom:** a TV show about characters in different comedic situations

Will and Jada met in 1994. Jada auditioned to play his girlfriend on the hit series *The Fresh Prince of Bel-Air*. Jada is 5 feet tall. She was considered too short to work with the 6-foot, 2-inch star. She didn't get the part.

In 1997, Will and Jada were married. Will already had one son, Trey, with his first wife. Then Jaden Christopher Syre was born in 1998. Willow Camille Reign was born on Halloween in 2000.

**Robsol Pinkett Jr.**
*July 14, 1952–February 20, 2010*
construction business owner

**Adrienne Banfield-Jones**
*October 18, 1953*
nurse and talk show host

**Jada Pinkett-Smith**
*September 18, 1971*
actress, singer, writer, producer, and talk show host

**Jaden Christopher Syre Smith**
*July 9, 1998*
actor, musician, model, and activist

**Willow Camille Reign Smith**
*October 31, 2000*
actor, model, and talk show host

# Chapter 3

# THE NEXT GENERATION

Jaden got an early start in show business. When he was only eight, he starred with Will in *The Pursuit of Happyness*. The movie is based on the life of **entrepreneur** Chris Gardner. The man was homeless for a short time. Will said that working with his son made it easier to play the role. He could imagine how Gardner worried about taking care of his own family. Will and Jaden made another movie together. It was the 2013 sci-fi film *After Earth*.

Jaden filmed *The Karate Kid* with action star Jackie Chan in China. Jaden was 11. He learned kung fu and performed his own stunts in the film. He also learned enough Mandarin to respond to his kung fu teacher. Mandarin is a language spoken in China. Jaden has mostly been **homeschooled**. This way, he can travel and build his own career.

**entrepreneur:** someone who starts a business and takes on large financial risk to do so

**homeschool:** a style of education where parents teach their children at home

Jackie Chan praised Jaden for his martial arts and stunts abilities. "He's very, very good," Chan said. "I think he was born like that, he has this kind of gene, like me!"

In addition to the arts, Willow is interested in science, particularly physics. "I can have the best of both worlds," she said.

Like Jaden, Willow has also been mostly homeschooled. This makes her whirlwind career possible. Willow made headlines at age 10. They were for her first **single**, "Whip My Hair." The song and its music video went **viral**. Willow was one of the youngest artists to sign with rapper Jay-Z's **record label** Roc Nation.

Early in her career, many of Willow's projects involved her parents. She appeared in *I Am Legend* with Will in 2007. She joined Jada as a **voiceover** actor. In 2008's *Madagascar: Escape 2 Africa*, Willow played a baby hippo. Also in 2008, she appeared in *Kit Kittredge: An American Girl*. The film is about a young girl in the 1930s.

**single:** one song either released by itself, or as part of a larger musical album

**viral:** spread very quickly to many people, usually via the internet

**record label:** a company that helps musical artists produce, promote, and sell their music

**voiceover:** when only an actor's voice and not their face is used for a production, such as voice actors for animated films and TV shows

While Jaden and Willow spread their wings, parents Will and Jada did not slow down. Jada appeared in several films. She starred in the TV series *Hawthorne* from 2009 to 2011. Will continued his blockbuster career. He made 12 films between 2000 and 2010.

The busy Smith family even had an overlapping film debut. Willow's *Kit Kittredge* opened July 2, 2008. It was the same day Will's movie *Hancock* came out.

Although they are separated by two years, Willow and Jaden have said they feel like twins. "We're like binary stars, like two parts of one thing," Willow said.

## MUSICAL TALENTS

Though their acting careers receive a lot of attention, the Smith family shares an interest in music too. Jada is the lead singer of a **nü-metal** band called Wicked Wisdom. She has been performing with the group since 2002. In 1998, Will won a Grammy for his popular song, "Gettin' Jiggy Wit It." Trey recorded his first song with Will when he was five years old. It was called "Just the Two of Us."

**nü-metal:** a type of music that combines heavy metal with other music genres, such as hip-hop, alternative rock, and grunge

# Chapter 4

# SMITH FAMILY VALUES

The members of the Smith family are talented performers. But that's not the only thing that is important to them. Will, Jada, and their children like to help others achieve their dreams as well. They do this by being activists. They are also **philanthropists**. This means they donate money. Support is given to organizations that help others.

The Will and Jada Smith Family Foundation was started in 1996. Their mission is to "improve lives by creating opportunities for often unheard voices, inspiring communities to reach their full potential." The foundation supports causes that focus on arts and education. It also supports **social empowerment** and **sustainability**. Recipients are doing great things. They just need some help to reach their goals.

**philanthropist:** a rich person who gives money to help improve other people's lives

**social empowerment:** being able to take action and change society for the better

**sustainability:** the ability to use methods that do not destroy natural resources

Famous Fact

In 2009, the year President Barack Obama won the Nobel Peace Prize, Will and Jada co-hosted the Nobel Peace Prize Concert in Oslo, Norway.

In 2009, a Nobel Peace Prize official said the Smiths have had a "global impact on the arts and philanthropy."

In 2020 during the COVID-19 pandemic, the Smiths passed their time talking to guests remotely on Red Table Talk. Some of their topics included dealing with anxiety during the pandemic and the importance of flattening the curve. Red Table Talk was a nominee for Best Talk Show at the 2021 Critics' Choice Television Awards.

Jada also launched an all-natural cosmetics line in 2021. Hey Humans is a 20-item product line that includes toothpaste, body wash, and lotion. It is available only at Target.

During her Trailblazer Award speech, Jada said anyone can be a trailblazer by overcoming pain, uncertainty, and false beliefs within their own minds.

Like their parents, the Smith children think it's important to get involved. They are volunteers and activists. Jaden and Willow have served as youth **ambassadors** for Project Zambi. This program helps children in Africa whose families have been affected by AIDS. It is a serious and often deadly disease.

Jaden Smith also helps residents in Flint, Michigan. It is through a company he helped form called JUST Water. The water supply in the city has been contaminated. The water is dangerous to use. Jaden's organization works with a local church. They provide access to a portable **water treatment system**. JUST Water also provides bottled water. It comes in eco-friendly containers.

Jaden was upset by plastic bottle litter. He decided to do something about it. JUST Water bottles are mostly made of paper.

**ambassador:** someone who represents a group while living in another country

**water treatment system:** a system that takes dirty or undrinkable water and makes it safe to drink

## A FAMILY BUSINESS

The Smith family appeared on *The Oprah Winfrey Show* in 2010. They talked about their goals and achievements as a family unit. Will and Jada said that they make sure their children can explore and develop their talents. "Once we started to see how the children were growing and . . . becoming their own beings, we decided, 'Okay, we want to make a family business,'" Jada said. "So that's our vision—to create a place where their dreams can come true as well."

# Chapter 5

# A LOOK AHEAD

Millions of fans tune into Will's YouTube channel. They can watch all of his latest updates. Many of the scenes on the YouTube channel feature the family relaxing. They hang out before and after big events. This includes movie premieres and award ceremonies. Viewers get to see the warm and supportive relationships the family shares. Fans can also watch the family joking together.

Will's most recent YouTube posts promote his latest projects. One is a *Fresh Prince of Bel-Air* reunion. Another is a Netflix series called *Amend*, a six-episode documentary about the 14th Amendment.

These clips earn millions of views. Fans comment on how much they enjoy getting to know the family better. This famous family continues to create and **collaborate** as actors, singers, and performers. They share their new projects on social media so their fans can stay connected.

---

**collaborate:** to work with another person or group in order to achieve a goal

---

*Famous Fact*

Jada's talk show, *Red Table Talk*, returned to Facebook Watch for a fourth season in March 2021.

---

Will and Jada have never appeared in a show or movie together, but they have produced many films through their production company, Overbrook Entertainment.

The Smith clan keeps expanding their roles as artists and philanthropists. As the children grow into adults, they are expanding their careers too. Jaden continues to act and make music. In 2020, he appeared in the drama *Life in a Year*. He also released his third album in 2020. The title is *CTV3: Cool Tape Vol. 3*. Willow also released an album in 2020. It is her fourth album. It is called *The Anxiety*.

Trey and his mother Sheree are very much in the family fold. Trey is an actor and DJ. He is based in Los Angeles. Sheree supports Jada's and Willow's work. She was the first guest on their Facebook talk show. The family will continue to come together to share and celebrate each other's successes.

Will starred in the movie *Bad Boys for Life* in 2020. He also has several new movies in the works. One is called *King Richard*. He will play Richard Williams. Richard is the father of tennis stars Venus and Serena Williams. In the film, he portrays a dad coaching his children. Richard helps them follow their passions. He guides them toward success. It is the perfect role for Will.

The family supported Will at his premiere for *Gemini Man* in 2019.

## APRIL FOOL'S JOKE

The Smith family are sports fans too! They root for Will's home team, the Philadelphia 76ers. On April Fool's Day in 2016, a hoax was spread online that Will and Jada were going to take over the team as majority owners. But it was just a joke. Their role is small, and they are only part owners with a large **investment group**. The couple loves the team, and they attend games when they can.

**investment group:** a group of people who all chip in a certain amount of money to make a larger profit

## 1986

Rapper Will Smith and his friend and performing partner DJ Jazzy Jeff Townes release their single, "Girls Ain't Nothing but Trouble." It lands in the top 60 of the Billboard Hot 100 music chart.

## 1994

Will and Jada meet on the set of *The Fresh Prince of Bel-Air*.

## 1997

Will and Jada get married on New Year's Eve. Jada becomes stepmother to Will's first son, Trey.

## 2014

Jada begins her role as Fish Mooney on *Gotham*, a fantasy-crime television series on Fox. She plays the part until 2017.

## 2021

*Red Table Talk*, which is the number one original series on Facebook Watch, returns for a fourth season.

## 2010

Willow's song "Whip My Hair" is on the Billboard Hot 100 music chart, which tracks the most popular songs. The single is on the chart for 12 weeks, reaching a peak position of 13.

## 2018

Will celebrates his 50th birthday by bungee jumping out of a helicopter above the Grand Canyon. Will says he did it because he was afraid to do it. He wanted to overcome his fear.

# Quiz

**1** What is the name of the movie in which Will Smith played a genie?

**2** What was the name of the show where Will and Jada first met?

**3** Where did Jada Pinkett-Smith attend school?

**4** For which two movies did Will Smith receive Academy Award nominations?

**5** In which movie do both Jada and Willow appear as voiceover actors?

**6** What song did Will record with his five-year-old son Trey?

**7** What is the name of the foundation that Jaden formed to help the residents of Flint, Michigan?

**8** What is the name of the talk show that Jada hosts along with her mother and daughter?

**1.** *Aladdin*

**2.** *The Fresh Prince of Bel-Air*

**3.** Baltimore School for the Arts

**4.** *The Pursuit of Happyness* and *Ali*

**5.** *Madagascar: Escape 2 Africa*

**6.** "Just the Two of Us"

**7.** JUST Water

**8.** *Red Table Talk*

# *Activity*

The Smith family looks for ways to donate their time and resources to causes they feel are important. What is important to you? How can you get involved and make things better in your community?

## MATERIALS

- pen and pencil
- local newspaper
- internet access
- helpful adult

## STEPS

1. Make a list of ways you would like to help your community. Do you care deeply about animals? Are you concerned about pollution? Read your list and decide which item is a top priority.

2. Read your local newspaper or check out your town or city's website page. Are there any organizations, such as an animal shelter, that are looking for help? Are there any events happening, like a community cleanup, that you could attend?

3. With an adult's help, reach out to the group whose goals match your values. Ask questions in an email or on the phone about the work they do. Learn more and decide if you'd like to get involved.

4. Participate in an event—a fundraiser, a walk to raise awareness, or any kind of community event. Share this experience with an adult.

5. Write a reflection of your experience. Decide if you want to continue working with the group, or research another way to give back to your community. Have fun sharing your talents and skills with others!

# Glossary

**activist:** someone who works to support change in society

**ambassador:** someone who represents a group while living in another country

**collaborate:** to work with another person or group in order to achieve a goal

**DJ:** someone who plays recorded music on a radio show or at a public gathering

**entrepreneur:** someone who starts a business and takes on large financial risk to do so

**homeschool:** a style of education where parents teach their children at home

**investment group:** a group of people who all chip in a certain amount of money to make a larger profit

**nü-metal:** a type of music that combines heavy metal with other music genres, such as hip-hop, alternative rock, and grunge

**philanthropist:** a rich person who gives money to help improve other people's lives

**premiere:** the first time a movie or TV show is shown

**record label:** a company that helps musical artists produce, promote, and sell their music

**single:** one song either released by itself, or as part of a larger musical album

**sitcom:** a TV show about characters in different comedic situations

**social empowerment:** being able to take action and change society for the better

**sustainability:** the ability to use methods that do not destroy natural resources

**taskmaster:** someone who assigns difficult work to other people

**viral:** spread very quickly to many people, usually via the internet

**voiceover:** when only an actor's voice and not their face is used for a production, such as voice actors for animated films and TV shows

**water treatment system:** a system that takes dirty or undrinkable water and makes it safe to drink

**work ethic:** the idea that hard work is a good thing

# Read More

*Careers: The Graphic Guide to Planning Your Future.* New York: DK Children, 2015.

**Clinton, Chelsea.** *Start Now!* You Can Make a Difference. New York: Philomel, 2018.

**Golkar, Golriz.** *Jaden Smith.* North Mankato, MN: Capstone Press, 2018.

**Nardo, Don.** Careers in Film, TV, and Theater. San Diego, CA: ReferencePoint Press, 2020.

**Schuman, Michael.** *Will Smith: A Biography of a Rapper Turned Movie Star.* Berkeley Heights, NJ: Enslow Publishers, Inc., 2013.

# Internet Sites

**Famous Birthdays**
*Willow has a famous birthday. Find out more!*
https://www.famousbirthdays.com/people/willow-smith.html

**Jada Pinkett-Smith Biography**
*Learn more about Jada Pinkett-Smith's life and career.*
https://www.biography.com/actor/jada-pinkett-smith

**Jaden Smith Biography**
*Learn more about Jaden Smith's life and career.*
https://www.biography.com/musician/jaden-smith

**Kids Fun Facts**
*Discover fun facts about Will Smith's career.*
http://www.fun-facts.org.uk/black-americans/will-smith.htm

# Index